ARDUTHIE SCHOOL
ARDUTHIE ROAD
STONEHAVEN AB39 2DP
Tel: 01569 762996

Fish

with Grog

Cutlass

Bilge

Step aboard one of the smallest ships on the high seas and meet the crew.

Grog

Swab

Cat

Rats

Jones

Booty

Flamingo

Poop

It's a fine and sunny day
aboard The Rubber Duck.

"Ahoy," says Grog happily as he opens the oven door and takes out a hot pizza. Grog puts on his special pizza-cutting attachment and spins it proudly. He cuts the pizza carefully into big juicy slices.

Grog puts the plate of pizza in the lift and sends
it upstairs.
"**Ding!**" the lift arrives. Swab takes the plate.
"**Yoho!**" Swab says hungrily. It smells yummy.

Swab puts a slice of pizza on everyone's plate.
Swab and Bilge eat quickly. But Cutlass doesn't want
pizza. She pushes it away and makes a face.

Cutlass pulls out a crayon.
"**Yoho**," she says thoughtfully. She draws on her napkin. Then she folds it up and sends it down in the lift to Grog.

Grog opens the napkin.
Cutlass has drawn a fish.

Grog looks at Cutlass's drawing and goes to the cupboard. He opens the flap with a blue fish on. He pulls out, not a fish but, a … fishing rod!

Cutlass dangles her new fishing rod out of the window. She is still hungry and wants to catch her supper.

Grog looks out of the galley window and sees
Cutlass has caught a starfish on her line.
Cutlass is very disappointed not to catch a fish.
She throws the starfish back into the sea.

The next time Grog looks out of his window, he sees that Cutlass has caught a shell, not a fish.

"**Ahoy**," Grog exclaims. He has an idea. He puts Cutlass's drawing of a fish over the pizza and traces the shape. He puts on his pizza-cutting attachment and gets to work.

When the fishing hook goes past the window for the third time, Grog catches the line and pulls it into the galley. He puts something special on the hook.

Up on the deck, Bilge and Swab are helping Cutlass pull.
"**Oooooff!**" They all pull together.

They think they must have caught a huge fish.

Grog lets go of the hook and the line whizzes away through the window. Bilge, Swab and Cutlass are still tugging so hard that they fall on their bottoms.

Cutlass looks at her hook. She's caught a pizza-fish! **"Yoho,"** she says happily.

Cutlass settles down to eat her supper at last.
Grog comes up to the deck carrying a plate of
warm biscuits.

Clever Grog has cut out biscuits shaped like the starfish and the shell that Cutlass caught. He gives one to Bilge and Swab.

Cutlass is delighted with her pizza-fish.

She takes a great big bite of cheesey, tomatoey fish!